The Reek from Outer Space

By Katherine Pebley O'Neal

Illustrated by Daryll Collins

ALADDIN PAPERBACKS
New York   London   Toronto   Sydney   Singapore

Dedicated to my wonderful family —K. P. O.

*To Jason, Rachel, Kara, Ryan,
Missy, and Trevor —D. C.*

First Aladdin Paperbacks edition June 2003

Text copyright © 2003 by Katherine Pebley O'Neal
Illustrations copyright © 2003 by Daryll Collins

ALADDIN PAPERBACKS
An imprint of Simon & Schuster
Children's Publishing Division
1230 Avenue of the Americas
New York, NY 10020

Designed by Sammy Yuen Jr.
The text of this book was set in font Century ITC.

Printed in the United States of America
2 4 6 8 10 9 7 5 3 1
Library of Congress Control Number 2002115507
ISBN 0-689-85699-7

Chapter One
Space Invaders?

"There's nothing quite like the sweet smell of success, right, Whiff?" Gilbreath said to his trusty bloodhound. They had just helped save the world from stench and were ready to relax in Dr. Shroeder's fragrant cabin high in the mountains.

Nine-year-old Gilbreath inhaled with joy. The wonderful aroma of sizzling bacon, hot blueberry pancakes, and thick maple syrup floated from the kitchen.

Suddenly, a strong odor, like fruit punch syrup, sliced through the air.

"Smellophone," Dr. Shroeder called, from the leather chair by the fireplace.

Gilbreath lifted the receiver. A wave of stench

washed over him, and then was gone. A frantic voice explained the reason for the call.

"It's for you, Uncle Shroeder!" Gilbreath reported to his famous uncle. "It's NASA calling. The Hubbel Smelloscope is detecting mysterious odors from outer space. And whew, do they stink!" Gilbreath held the smellophone away from his nose.

"Alien odors," Dr. Shroeder said thoughtfully, taking the phone. "Thank you, Gilbreath."

Gilbreath's uncle Shroeder was a well-known odorologist and the world's leading Private Nose. Gilbreath was lucky to be able to spend time with his famous uncle while his parents were traveling around the world.

"Smells from outer space, Whiff!" Gilbreath said, nose to nose with his best friend. "Do you think they're friendly odors? What if it's a stink attack?"

"Woof!" Whiff said. He was balancing their red plastic snozbee on his furry wet nose.

"You're right, Whiff," said Gilbreath. "Let's go outside. Uncle Shroeder might be on the phone for a long time."

They headed out into the crisp autumn air.

A sharp apple scent of bubbling cider and a spicy hot aroma of chili floated up from the valley below. The dusty fresh smell of new hay bales and the polished wood fragrance of fiddles told Gilbreath their hillbilly neighbors were getting ready for the annual Toot 'n' Nanny smellabration. Gilbreath took a deep breath. The odors made him forget about the outer space smells for a minute. "I can't wait for the Toot 'n' Nanny, Whiff!" Gilbreath said excitedly to his pal. "There's going to be a hoedown square dance and hay rides, not to mention the Toot 'n' Nanny smellabration itself, which can get pretty stinky!" He tugged his nose. "And this year, I signed us up for our first Sniff-Off, for the best all-around smell. I already started putting our entry together, with our favorite scents: Birthday Cake and Ice Cream!"

"Woof!" said Whiff. He twirled the plastic

snozbee on his warm, furry nose and sent it sailing toward Gilbreath.

The snozbee sailed over Gilbreath's upturned nose into a thick lilac bush.

"I got it!" Gilbreath called, following the snozbee with an impressive nosedive. But the next instant, the bush exploded with the odor of angry skunk.

"Ooh, that reeks!" Gilbreath adjusted his glasses. "I guess I should have sniffed before I leaped. Whew-ee!"

"Woof!" apologized Whiff.

Gilbreath took a deep breath to clear his nose, and inhaled fragrances of autumn leaves and crisp mountain air. A scent heaven for an odorologist-in-training and his trusty bloodhound.

"Just take a sniff, Whiff!" Gilbreath said. "We could use all of these wonderful fragrances for our entry in the Sniff-Off. Except Angry Skunk, of course. Whew! Let's go inside."

Dr. Shroeder was still on the smellophone with the Space Scenter. Strange odors had been detected by the Hubbel Smelloscope and the baffled astronomers had automatically called the famous odorologist. Where were the odors coming from? What did they mean? Why did they stink?

"We'll be there right away!" Dr. Shroeder hung up the smellophone and turned to Gilbreath. "Pack up our gear and load the sno-tomobile, Gilbreath. The scientists at the Space Scenter need our help! Once again, the fate of the world depends on us."

Chapter Two
Loading the Snotomobile

*G*ilbreath tugged at his modest nose. He could smell the burned wood in the cabin's stone fireplace, the delicate papery fragrance of the hundreds of books that lined the cabin walls, and the rich leather aroma from his uncle's favorite overstuffed chair.

Gilbreath carefully removed their scent detection gear from a big cedar-lined closet. Most important was the Odor Decoder, a pocket-sized gadget that Dr. Shroeder had invented to analyze scents with pinpoint accuracy. Gilbreath polished it on his shirt front. *Breakfast Pancake Syrup, Grass Clippings, Sweat Drops, Snozbee Plastic, Angry Skunk,* the Decoder readout reported.

"Oops," said Gilbreath. "Guess I forgot to turn it off. Maybe I'd better change my shirt."

Next he packed the Odor Unloader, which was big and awkward, like a vacuum cleaner, with bottles of all sizes for capturing and storing odors, along with all its attachments.

Gilbreath tugged at his nose as he packed a different gadget. "Here's Uncle Shroeder's latest invention, Whiff," he explained. "It's an Odor Emoter. It translates feelings and emotions into smell! Let's test it."

Gilbreath typed in HAPPY on the keypad, pointing the gadget at himself. The Emoter gurgled for

a minute, considering its subject. Then it slowly released the fresh scent of Saturday morning in spring, the exciting odor of skateboard sparks, the spicy fragrance of cheese pizza, and the sugary smell of birthday cake and ice cream. "Smells pretty *happy* to me," Gilbreath said with a big smile.

"Woof!" said Whiff.

"Okay, we'll try it on you, Whiff." Gilbreath typed in HAPPY again, pointing the Emoter at his pal. The gadget bubbled and popped as it calculated canine scents, then emitted the soft fragrance of a good scratch behind the ears, the musty odor of a bone buried in the backyard, the plastic smell of a chewed-up snozbee, and the sugary scent of birthday cake and ice cream.

"See?" said Gilbreath. "It's so easy to use—all you do is point! It can even take in odors and tell how someone is feeling. Let's try it on me."

The Emoter gurgled as it pulled in the

emotional odors coming from Gilbreath, then translated them into odors they could identify. Out popped the sticky scent of cotton candy, the metallic odor of roller-coaster steel, the freshness of whipping wind. The Emoter screen lit up with the word EXCITEMENT.

"That's right, Whiff!" said Gilbreath. "I'm excited about working on a new case with Uncle Shroeder! What a great invention!" he exclaimed.

A separate case held Gilbreath's own invention supplies, including the white glass bottle that held their Sniff-Off entry.

Gilbreath carried the bags out to the snotomobile. This was a vehicle that ran on a secret fuel discovered by Gilbreath during a bad head cold. It worked well and was dependable.

"Is everything ready, Gilbreath?" Dr. Shroeder asked, climbing into the driver's seat. "The Space Scenter is depending on us to analyze the mysterious odor waves from space. We won't let them down."

Chapter Three
He Who Smelt It, Dealt It

Sputtering along in the snotomobile a short time later, Gilbreath detected the musty odor of fresh hay piled along the road side.

A sign nearby read: WARNING! THIS AREA RATED "R—REPULSIVE" BY THE SCENT SOCIETY. ODORS UNSUITABLE FOR SENSITIVE NOSES.

"Look, Uncle Shroeder, the Hillbillies are getting ready for the Annual Toot 'n' Nanny smellabration!" he exclaimed. "And the Scent Society has already been here," he added, nodding at the warning sign.

The pink, powdered Scent Society ladies fought a constant battle against foul odors, using methods that ranged from warning labels to protest marches. They would do almost anything to destroy offensive smells. They were making sure the Toot 'n' Nanny didn't get out of hand.

Gilbreath saw a big red barn ahead of them.

"There's old Rip Corncob, flagging us down," said Dr. Shroeder. He pulled the snotomobile over to greet a bearded man in a red plaid shirt, tattered overalls, and a well-worn straw hat.

"Yee haw! Well, if it ain't Doc Shroeder and the young 'un. How are ya?" asked Rip Corncob. He slapped Dr. Shroeder on the back. "It's a rib-tickler of a treat to see ya'll!"

"We're doing very well, Rip," Dr. Shroeder replied, slapping him back in a traditional hillbilly greeting. "We can only stop for a moment. How is the Toot 'n' Nanny coming?"

"Oh, Doc! We're gearing up for a gut-buster of a good time. We got the pre–Toot 'n' Nanny banquet just about set up and ready to go. It's gonna be a lip-smacker of a feast," boasted Rip.

Gilbreath sniffed. He detected odors of chili powder, barbecue sauce, and too many types of beans to count.

"Look here, Doc," continued Rip. "We got yer

double bean hillbilly chili, jalapeño bean burri-
tos, creamy butter-bean soup, fresh bean sprout
salad, tangy oven-baked barbecue beans, corn
chip bean dip, smooth lima beans au gratin, and
tutti-frutti jelly beans to top it all off. It's gonna
be a rip-roarin' smellabration. Them beans'll
put the TOOT in Toot 'n' Nanny, that's for dern
sure. Will you join us for the banquet?"

"Thank you, Rip, but we can't," declined Dr.
Shroeder. "We are in a hurry. You see, smells
seem to be coming from outer space."

"Smells? Outer space? Well, that's a real brainteaser of a situation, Doc."

"I'm sure there's a simple explanation," said Dr. Shroeder. "We'll find it and be back in time for the smellabration."

"I hear Gilbreath is signed up for his first Sniff-Off that the Scent Society holds every year. Miss Lilly says we got to balance the Toot 'n' Nanny with some nice smells." He paused. "Of course, if it was up to the Scent Society, there'd be no Toot 'n' Nanny at all!"

Gilbreath tugged at his nose. "Yes, sir," he replied. "We're hoping for the blue ribbon."

"Good luck, son," said Rip. "That's gonna be a nose-blower of a competition. Moose has been preparing nonstop since last year."

Rip nodded in the direction of the barn. A kid, wearing a red baseball cap covered with blue ribbons, was twirling a snozbee on a huge gold trophy. Moose had clearly won the Sniff-Off many years in a row.

"Moose was also last year's Toot 'n' Nanny Top Tooter," Rip Corncob said with pride. "Ya'll can see the Top Tooter Trophy for yourselves."

On cue, a loud noise erupted from Moose's direction. "Excuse me!" Moose called with a smile that revealed a chipped front tooth.

Gilbreath and Whiff had to hold their breath to keep from giggling out loud, which luckily kept them from inhaling the stink that followed.

"Did you see all those blue ribbons?" Gilbreath whispered to Whiff. He pulled out the Odor Emoter and pointed it at himself.

Out flowed the salty odor of forehead sweat, the light, fluttery fragrance of butterflies, the thick, heavy aroma of pressure.

"Smell that, Whiff?" asked Gilbreath. "I feel nervous!" The Odor Emoter screen confirmed Gilbreath's emotion in red letters.

Whiff covered his head with his paw.

Chapter Four

Scent Society Sabotage

"Don't be nervous about the Sniff-Off, Gilbreath," Dr. Shroeder advised. They had left the Hillbillies behind and continued on to the Space Scenter. "Use fragrances that you like, and the judges will like them too."

Gilbreath pulled his nose. He wasn't so sure.

Suddenly both Gilbreath and his uncle were distracted by a strong perfume.

Wafting from a bush up ahead was a powdery cloud that could only mean one thing: The Scent Society was nearby, on a mission to keep the world smelling fresh. Not wanting to go closer, they pulled off the road to watch from a distance.

Three plump women were hiding behind a bush near the hillbilly camp. They were dressed in overalls and straw hats, instead of their usual stylish pastel suits. But their shiny *S* pins, white gloves, and the heavy cloud of powders, lotions, and sprays gave them away. Miss Lilly and the Scent Society were up to something.

Gilbreath inhaled deeply. He could detect the potent odor of uncapped permanent markers, and the aroma of cardboard. He checked the Odor Decoder: *Ultra Black Highlighter, 24" by 40" Poster Board.* The Scent Society was planning a Toot 'n' Nanny protest march!

A hint of metal and plastic Baggies made Gilbreath take a closer sniff. The Decoder read,

Twelve-inch Metal Bean Tweezers, Special Odor Bag.

Bean Tweezers? Gilbreath thought for a minute. "Uncle Shroeder!" he said. "Do you think Miss Lilly is trying to de-bean the chili?"

"The Scent Society is up to its old tricks," Dr. Shroeder said. "Sponsoring the Sniff-Off isn't enough for Miss Lilly. She will do anything to keep the world smelling fresh."

Gilbreath faced his pal. "I don't think even Miss Lilly could get rid of every bean in that banquet, Whiff." He pushed up his glasses.

Suddenly, Dr. Shroeder was aware of another odor. "Gilbreath, did you get a whiff of that?"

Gilbreath inhaled nothing but powdery fluff. He pulled his nose.

"There it is again," Dr. Shroeder said. "It's faint, but foul."

Gilbreath sniffed again. He could just barely make out a far-off reek. Then it was gone.

"Maybe they're warming up for the Toot 'n' Nanny, Uncle Shroeder," Gilbreath guessed.

"Perhaps," Dr. Shroeder said with hesitation.

The foul odors came and went as they drove to the Space Scenter. Each pulse was stronger than the one before. Soon Gilbreath could smell the aroma waves with no trouble, just like his uncle. By the time they reached the lab, Dr. Shroeder was certain that the odors were from outer space—and now they were detectable without the use of the smelloscope!

Gilbreath saw with alarm that people on the street were noticing the odors. They looked up with wrinkled noses or covered their faces as each wave hit. He checked his watch. The odor waves were coming closer together than before—about fifteen minutes apart.

"Each pulsing odor is stronger, with a higher

stench level than the one before," Dr. Shroeder said thoughtfully as the snotomobile sputtered to a stop in front of a clean, white, dome-shaped building. A huge silver archway marked the Space Scenter entrance.

A jumpy man wearing a white lab coat that seemed to be on backward was pacing nervously. When he spotted Dr. Shroeder, Gilbreath, and Whiff, he nearly dropped his clipboard trying to flag them down.

"Dr. Shroeder?" he called. "Is that you? Thank goodness you're here. I'm Professor Blink. You're Dr. Shroeder. Where is my clipboard?"

"You're holding it," Gilbreath said helpfully.

Professor Blink looked down and was sur-prised at the sight of the clipboard clutched at his chest. "Here it is!" he cried. "Thank you!"

"Professor Blink, this is my nephew Gilbreath and his best friend, Whiff," Dr. Shroeder said.

"I'm Professor Blink," Professor Blink said. "You're Gilbreath and Whiff. Welcome to the Space Scenter."

While Professor Blink hurried them through the security check and up to the main lab, Gilbreath tested the Odor Emoter. The reading for Professor Blink was interesting: the soft fragrance of puzzle pieces, the magnetic odor of a spinning compass needle, the cool clay scent of a brick wall. Gilbreath had to check the Emoter display to be sure. It read: TOTAL CONFUSION.

"The odors are intensifying," Professor Blink explained. "What do these odors mean? Is someone trying to communicate with us? What are they saying? Where are my glasses?"

"Do you mean the ones on your head?" Gilbreath suggested.

Professor Blink reached up and touched his glasses with a start. "Here they are! Thank you, Gilbreath. And thank you for coming, Dr. Shroeder. We're fortunate to have an expert in the field of odorology."

"My pleasure," Dr. Shroeder answered. All

around them scientists nudged one another and stared. *It's the famous Dr. Shroeder!* Gilbreath looked at his uncle with pride.

"Wow, Whiff! Look at that huge smelloscope!" Gilbreath exclaimed to his pal.

The Hubbel Smelloscope's massive nostrils reached through an opening in the roof toward outer space. Gilbreath detected the fragrance of test-tube glass, and of course, the unpleasant odor waves coming from outer space.

"Our graph shows the rate of growing intensity," Professor Blink explained. He looked around wildly. "Where's our graph?"

"Is this it, behind you?" asked Gilbreath.

Professor Blink turned around. The sight of the graph made him jump. "Oh, yes, here it is! Thank you, Gilbreath."

A red line on the graph moved higher with each odor pulse. "But the alarming thing is," Professor Blink continued, "the odors are getting slightly more repulsive with each wave."

Gilbreath watched his uncle analyze the information from the Hubbel Smelloscope.

Fragrances of burning fuel, metallic tang, and a hint of lime slime convinced Dr. Shroeder of the existence of an alien spaceship.

Gilbreath pulled out the Odor Decoder. Most of the smells were foreign to the human nose, but no problem for the Decoder: *Stagnant Bog, Floating Space Reekage, Rotting Solar Muck, Meteor Sludge.*

"Let's review what we know, Gilbreath," Dr. Shroeder suggested. "The odors are frequent and pulsating. They are clearly coming from an alien spaceship. They are growing in intensity. They are growing in stinkage."

Suddenly, one of the odor pulses struck with enough force to draw the attention of every scientist in the room. The one that followed was stronger. Gilbreath checked his watch. The pulses were only five minutes apart. The smell of the next pulse caused Professor Blink, who was closest to the smelloscope, to stumble backward and trip over Whiff.

"Sorry, Whiff!" Professor Blink apologized. Gilbreath helped him to his feet.

Professor Blink checked himself over. "This is remarkable!" he cried. "The smell was so potent, it knocked my lab coat around backward!" He turned his jacket the right way and made a note on his clipboard.

"At this rate of reek acceleration, the odors will soon be overwhelming," Dr. Shroeder said thoughtfully. He took a deep breath. "These are no ordinary fragrances," he realized. "I recall hearing about odors like these through my work with FUNK—the Federation for Unlimited Nostril Knowledge. Professor Blink, Gilbreath, Whiff, these may be alien Stink Pots! This is undoubtedly an evil plot to rule the world."

"Alien Stink Pots?" Gilbreath whispered to Whiff.

"We don't know much about Alien Stink Pots," Dr. Shroeder continued, "except the possibility that they exist. We'll just have to play this by nose, and smell what happens."

"Oh, no! Not alien Stink Pots!" Professor Blink moaned.

"We may be able to hold them off, using the Odor Unloader," Dr. Shroeder speculated, "as long as we stop all Earthly stench during this crisis. A foul odor overload could mean the end of the world as we know it. Total odor annihilation. The world destroyed by stench."

A strong Stink Pot caused several scientists to spill their test tubes. The Decoder identified Mutant Mulch, Odoriferous Ozone, and Smelly Star Slurg wafting across the laboratory.

Suddenly, a horrible thought dawned on

Gilbreath. "What about the annual Hillbilly Toot 'n' Nanny!" he said.

Professor Blink turned pale. "Oh, no! Not the Toot 'n' Nanny!" he cried. Then he added quietly, "What is the Toot 'n' Nanny?"

"You must have heard of the Hillbilly Toot 'n' Nanny, Professor," said Gilbreath. "It's the famous annual smellabration where they eat as many beans as they can and then, well, as Mr. Corncob puts it, they let 'em rip."

Every scientist in the lab froze in horror.

"Oh, THAT Hillbilly Toot 'n' Nanny?" said Professor Blink. "With the alien Stink Pots—what terrible timing! That combination of odors could be lethal. We must find Dr. Shroeder!"

Professor Blink whipped around to find himself staring straight into Dr. Shroeder's massive nose. "There you are! We have an emergency!"

"I am aware, Professor Blink," Dr. Shroeder said thoughtfully. "Total odor annihilation. We've got to stop the Hillbillies. Gilbreath, get Rip Corncob on the smellophone!"

Chapter Six
An Unstoppable Stench

Gilbreath raced to the smellophone in the hall to alert the Hillbillies of the danger. Surely they would call off the Toot 'n' Nanny, and the world would be safe until Dr. Shroeder could stop the alien threat.

"Mr. Corncob!" Gilbreath shouted into the smellophone. "You've got to call off the Toot 'n' Nanny! There's a spaceship, and it's dropping Stink Pots, and the reek will destroy the world, and they're coming faster and stinkier and—"

"Whoa, young 'un," Rip Corncob said. "That's a tongue twister you got there. What's this about aliens, and calling off the Toot 'n' Nanny?"

Gilbreath slowed down to explain the danger as clearly as he could. He could hear Miss Lilly and the Scent Society in the background, protesting. "Stop the stench! Stop the stench!" they chanted. For once, he agreed with them.

"See, Mr. Corncob?" he said, "you have to call off the Toot 'n' Nanny before it's too late. The combination of the Stink Pots and the Toot 'n' Nanny could cause odor annihilation!"

"That's a brow-knitter of a problem," Rip explained. "You see, we already served the pre–Toot 'n' Nanny banquet. It's been eaten down to the very last bean. Even the ones those Society gals tried to steal from the chili! There's no stopping the Toot 'n' Nanny now. No sirree, no turning back. Once that meal is eaten, we sit back and wait for the festivities to begin."

"Oh, no!" wailed Gilbreath. Another Stink Pot shook the laboratory with the stench of slimy space slop and cosmic crater rot.

"Smells like it's gettin' started now, even though it's early. This is a head-scratcher—I didn't expect the smellabration to start so soon. Must've served some fast-actin' beans this year. Whoa! That was a humdinger!"

"Mr. Corncob, hold up the smellophone. I want to analyze that last odor," Gilbreath said.

The Odor Decoder printout confirmed Gilbreath's worst suspicion: *Slimy Space Slop, Cosmic Crater Rot.* The Toot 'n' Nanny hadn't started yet, after all. The Stink Pots had reached the Hillbillies.

"Mr. Corncob, that wasn't the Toot 'n' Nanny," Gilbreath tried to explain. "It was an alien Stink Pot!"

With another pulse, Gilbreath heard the phone bounce to the ground on Rip's end of the line. The Stink Pot stench nearly knocked the phone from Gilbreath's hand as well. Gilbreath glanced at his watch. The Stink Pots were coming four minutes apart.

"The reek is horrible, Gilbreath! Definitely a nose-pincher," he heard Rip Corncob gasp from far away. "It's makin' our bandannas sag and our hats droop. The whole dern barn is leanin' to the left! This isn't from any bean I ever—"

"Hold on, Mr. Corncob! Do what you can to stop the Toot 'n' Nanny, and we'll do what we can to stop the aliens."

There was no answer.

The next alien Stink Pot sent Gilbreath and Whiff spinning head on into each other. The horrible stink was making the paint peel off the Space Scenter walls. The scientists' framed diplomas came crashing to the floor. The air around Gilbreath and Whiff was turning green.

Gilbreath pushed up his glasses. "What are we going to do now, Whiff?" he said, nose to nose with his pal.

"Whowooooo," Whiff whined, his paw over his sensitive nose.

Chapter Seven

A Stinky Strategy

Gilbreath and Whiff dashed back to the lab. They were slowed down by a Stink Pot that sent them somersaulting over a lab counter. They recovered, and quickly gave Dr. Shroeder the bad news.

Reports began to come in to the Space Scenter from all over. Jolts of Rotten Space Garbage, Cosmic Diaper Sludge, and Darkside Moon Nargle were crashing into Earth. Gilbreath checked his watch. The Stink Pots were hitting three minutes apart! The combination with the potent Toot 'n' Nanny was more than Gilbreath could imagine.

"I should have realized the Toot 'n' Nanny would be an unstoppable stench," mused Dr.

Shroeder. "We must arm ourselves with portable odor neutralizers."

He produced a box of gadgets that looked like clothespins. Gilbreath passed them around to the Space Scenter lab technicians.

"These will only work to a degree," Dr. Shroeder explained, pinching the only size extra-large onto his massive proboscis. "But they will allow us some time to concentrate on the problem without passing out from the stench." They all ducked as another Stink Pot sent test tubes flying like missiles. The odorometer began to shake wildly.

"Why are the aliens dropping Stink Pots, anyway, Uncle Shroeder?" Gilbreath wondered, with a pull at his neutralizer-pinched nose. "What have we ever done to them?"

"For that answer, we must continue to follow our noses, because as you know, the nose knows," said Dr. Shroeder. "Since the Toot 'n' Nanny can't be stopped," he continued, "we must try an Odor Unloader de-odor defense."

"An Odor Unloader de-odor defense?" said Gilbreath. He followed his uncle out of the lab to the snotomobile.

"A classic reek counterattack move," Dr. Shroeder explained. "We'll pull the odors into range with the Odor Unloader and deodorize them immediately with the de-odor attachment."

Gilbreath helped his uncle pull the heavy Odor Unloader from the snotomobile. He checked the running printout from the Decoder in his pocket: *Atrocious Astro Grunge, Grody Galaxy Gunk, Blucky Blast-off Barf.* Each Stink Pot odor landed harder and exploded with increased alien stench.

"We'll need all available deodorizers, Gilbreath," Dr. Shroeder was explaining. "There's a Nose Mart across the street. Gather all the deodorant they have—tell them it's an odor emergency. I'll have the Unloader ready when you return."

"Sure thing, Uncle Shroeder!" said Gilbreath. "Let's go, Whiff!"

"Woof!" Whiff responded, closing his portable odor neutralizer as tightly as he could over his wet nose with a furry paw.

Chapter Eight
The Nose Mart

As they entered the Nose Mart, they were greeted by a horrible mess. The once fragrant shelves and displays had been crushed to the floor with each Stink Pot strike. The smells clerk was on hands and knees, bravely trying to restore order to the lovely store, but each pulse of the alien Stink Pots sent him sprawling into the potpourri.

"Th-thank you for p-picking the N-Nose Mart," his voice quivered. "M-may I help you find s-something?"

"Yes, we need all of your—,"Gilbreath began.

"E-everything is in d-disarray because of this h-horrible stench," the smells clerk interrupted. Just then, a Stink Pot sent them all flying into a

stack of nose hair trimmers. A booger picker
3000 flew past Gilbreath and crashed into the
air fresheners.

"That's why we need all of your—," Gilbreath
started.

"The st-stink has destroyed almost everything. What are you l-looking for?"

"The stink is why we—," Gilbreath tried.

"Most of our b-best-selling items are on the
floor. Do you s-see what you're l-looking for?"

"JUST TELL ME WHERE YOU KEEP THE DEODORANT!" yelled Gilbreath.

"Of course. Why didn't you just say so?" sniffed the smells clerk. A pounding Stink Pot exploded with such force that the display counters along the wall came crashing down, flinging bottles and tubes and sprays everywhere. "There is the deodorant, now," the clerk said, ducking to avoid being hit by a roll-on antiperspirant.

"Thank you," said Gilbreath. "We'll take your entire inventor—"

"Th-thank you for p-picking the Nose Mart!"

said the smells clerk. "Have a good day!"

Gilbreath gathered up all the deodorants he could, quickly paid, and hurried back to the lab with Whiff. Stink Pot destruction was all around them. Flowers and trees were drooping. People were passed out along the sidewalk. The corners of buildings were starting to melt. The alien danger was becoming very serious.

"We bought all the deodorants they had, Uncle Shroeder," Gilbreath reported when they arrived.

"Good work, Gilbreath," said Dr. Shroeder. "It's time for roll-on retaliation."

"**W**e're going to deodorize the alien Stink
Pots, Professor Blink," explained Dr.
Shroeder. "We'll need to aim our Odor Unloader
hose through your smelloscope."

Gilbreath helped his uncle attach the Odor
Unloader to the base of the smelloscope. They
hooked the de-odor attachment into place and
Gilbreath loaded the chamber with the deodorant. Dr. Shroeder turned the Unloader on high.

When the next Stink Pot hit, the Unloader
sucked the stench within close range. Then the
de-odor attachment sent a cloud of baby powder-
fresh deodorant into the air after it. POW! The
deodorant crashed into the Stink Pot with a force
that shook the atmosphere.

But the Stink Pot reek remained! Dr. Shroeder tried again with the next attack. The Unloader pulled the stink with all its force, then the de-odor attachment puffed the air with a cloud of double-strength sport antiperspirant. Crash! But the stench still swirled around them.

"The Unloader can't pull in all the stink. It isn't powerful enough." Dr. Shroeder sighed. "The Stink Pots are too massive for the Unloader's suction power. Even the Odor Unloader de-odor defense can't stop this," he said.

Now the Stink Pots were landing harder and faster. Gilbreath checked his watch. Only one minute apart. Amazingly, he was able to detect the sharp scent of fruit punch syrup slicing through the alien stench. "Smellophone, Professor Blink," Gilbreath announced.

Professor Blink looked around wildly. "The smellophone! Where is the smellophone?"

"I'll get it," Gilbreath said helpfully, running out into the hallway. He lifted the receiver. "Space Scenter. May I help you?" he said.

The Stink Pot stench doubled in strength as it wafted from the smellophone nosepiece. Gilbreath tightened his portable odor neutralizer and pushed up his glasses. The reek was making his eyes water. "Hello?" he said.

"Howdy . . . gasp . . . young 'un!" said a weak Rip Corncob. "We're getting hit hard. Can't breathe . . . a real . . . gasp . . . heart-stopper of a situation. The alien spaceship . . . it's hovering just above the Toot 'n' Nanny . . . gasp. . . . The

Stink Pots are about to put us all away . . . so . . . gasp . . . we're gonna fight stench with reek. We're startin' the Toot 'n' Nanny, and we're aimin' high!"

Gilbreath could detect the reek of beans wafting through the smellophone nosepiece, followed by noises that sounded like a honking moose herd.

"No, Mr. Corncob!" warned Gilbreath. "That's just the opposite of what you should do! The combination of the Stink Pots and the Toot 'n' Nanny could cause total odor annihilation!"

"Well, we got a . . . gasp . . . nose-burner of a problem, 'cause we're not gonna last much longer. It's unbearable! Aauuugh!" Gilbreath heard the smellophone fall to the ground.

He had to alert Uncle Shroeder right away! He ran back into the lab.

The Odor Decoder identified alien stinks never before encountered by the human nose:

Potent Planet Puke, Smelly Space Spew, Gross Gravitational Gargle. He looked at his watch—thirty seconds between each hit!

"Uncle Shroeder!" Gilbreath reported. "The Hillbillies can see the spaceship. Mr. Corncob says it's hovering over the Toot 'n' Nanny!"

Gilbreath explained everything else Rip Corncob had said.

"If only we could communicate with them, Uncle Shroeder," Gilbreath said, tugging at his nose. "We could let them know we're friendly. We could make a peace offering or something."

"That's it, Gilbreath!" Dr. Shroeder looked at his nephew with pride. "A peace offering is a great idea, but it will be difficult to put together peaceful fragrances in the midst of this potent stench." He paused. "Gilbreath! How about your Sniff-Off entry for the Toot 'n' Nanny?"

"I don't know, Uncle Shroeder." Gilbreath hesitated, pushing his glasses up his nose. "It's not actually finished. . . ."

"It's a good place to start, Gilbreath," Dr. Shroeder reassured him. "Come with us,

Professor Blink. We'll need your help too."

"Oh, my. Oh, my!" Professor Blink began running around the lab, grabbing equipment and papers. "Where is my clipboard? Where is my calculator? Where is my pocket smelloscope? Where is the door?"

"Right this way, Professor Blink," Gilbreath said, opening the Space Scenter door for him.

"Of course. Thank you, Gilbreath," Professor Blink said. He followed Dr. Shroeder to the snoto-mobile. Gilbreath and Whiff quickly packed up the scent detection equipment. There was no break between Stink Pots now. With watering eyes, Gilbreath tightened his odor neutralizer and headed for the snotomobile.

"What an amazing vehicle," Professor Blink commented. "How does it work?"

"It runs on a secret fuel additive Gilbreath discovered," Dr. Shroeder explained.

"During a bad cold," added Gilbreath.

"Woof-CHOO!" Whiff sneezed.

"Nice illustration," Gilbreath said, handing him a tissue.

Chapter Ten

A Peace Offering

"Let's review your Sniff-Off entry so far, Gilbreath," Dr. Shroeder said as he drove. He had to steer the snotomobile around Stink Pot–flattened street signs and fallen tree limbs.

Gilbreath lifted the white bottle carefully from his inventions case, removed his odor neutralizer for a moment, and took a whiff. The sweet, sugary aroma was a relief in the midst of the Stink Pot stench all around them. He quickly capped the bottle and pinched the neutralizer back onto his nose. "We started with our favorites, Birthday Cake and Ice Cream— right Whiff?"

"Woof!" wagged Whiff.

"Then we added every great scent we could think of, odors that meant a lot to us—just like you suggested, Uncle Shroeder," Gilbreath explained. The Odor Decoder printout named each one: *Cozy Campfire, New Library Book Pages, Bicycle Tire Rubber, Hot Cheese Pizza, Soccer Ball Leather, Summer Thunderstorm, Snozbee Plastic, Picnic on Freshly Cut Grass, Steak Bone in Doggie Bag.*

"Whiff insisted on that last one," Gilbreath explained.

"A few more scents will make it clearly an offering of peace," suggested Dr. Shroeder. "Gilbreath, I believe there is an OlFactory fragrance sampler with the Unloader. It should give us a tiny sample of each scent in my OlFactory collection."

Gilbreath pulled the sampler from the bag. There were scents of every kind, ranging from Day-Old Diaper to Fresh-Spun Cotton Candy. Gilbreath studied them carefully. "How about White Dove Down, Uncle Shroeder?" he suggested. "That's peaceful. And maybe Vanilla

Candle, Clear Mountain Stream—or, I know, Olive Branch."

"Those will be very suitable," agreed Dr. Shroeder.

"Don't forget the wonderful aromas of starched lab coat and new graph paper!" said Professor Blink.

They all looked at Professor Blink. Dr. Shroeder cleared his throat.

"Okay . . . ," said Gilbreath.

Driving along, they could see more devastation left by the alien Stink Pots. The highway was curled up at the edges, and the smellophone poles drooped to the ground. Cows along the roadside had fallen over, feet in the air. Hay bales had melted into little piles of straw. There was a definite green cast to the air.

Suddenly a huge metal sphere could be seen ahead, floating toward the ground. Its dome reflected the green cloud that floated around it, and it seemed to be dripping something. Gilbreath removed his odor neutralizer again. He could clearly detect the metallic tang of the spaceship mixed with the constant Stink Pot pulsations. To make things worse, he could smell that the Toot 'n' Nanny had definitely begun.

He slipped his neutralizer onto his nose just in time to keep from being knocked over by the stench. The peace offering would have to work. There was no other option.

Professor Blink enclosed the peace offering aroma bottle in a pollution shield taken from the Space Scenter to keep it safe from stench. They arrived at the Toot 'n' Nanny site just as the spaceship reached the ground.

"There's the spaceship!" cried Professor Blink. "Where's my camera? Where's my smelloscope? Where's my odor neutralizer?"

"Is that your neutralizer, in your pocket?" offered Gilbreath.

Professor Blink looked at his pocket with surprise. "Here it is! Thank you, Gil—," he started, but the stench knocked him out before he could clip the neutralizer onto his nose.

In fact, everywhere they looked, people were fainting from the stench. Gilbreath recognized

Moose, collapsed in a pile of blue ribbons, and Mr. Corncob, passed out with the smellophone still clutched in his hand.

"Gilbreath, this aromatic peace offering is our only chance," said Dr. Shroeder. "Wish me luck." Gilbreath quickly checked the new Odor Emoter. The scents coming from his uncle clearly represented only one emotion: complete confidence. Gilbreath pushed up his glasses and breathed a sigh of relief. The world could depend on his famous uncle.

Just then a billowy perfumed puff could be barely detected over the awful Toot and Stink Pot combination, alerting Gilbreath and Dr.

Shroeder that the Scent Society was still on the scene. They spotted Miss Lilly and the other pastel ladies, all protected by pink gas masks decorated with a shiny gold *S* on the sides. The Scent Society had abandoned the protest march to help the passed-out Hillbillies.

Miss Lilly was dashing from victim to victim, trying her best to revive each one with smelling salts, scented sprays, perfumes, and encouragement. It was a brave effort, but mostly unsuccessful, since the victims passed out again as soon as they came to. There simply were not enough gas masks or odor neutralizers to go around. Miss Lilly was wiping her damp forehead with her white-gloved hand when she spotted Dr. Shroeder. She looked immensely relieved.

"Sniffton, dear!" she gushed. "What a relief to see you. This has been awful!" She rushed toward Dr. Shroeder with her gloved hand extended, and before

Dr. Shroeder could react, he was pulled into the huge powdery bear hug. By the time Miss Lilly released the crumpled odorologist, his extra-large odor neutralizer had been flung to the ground a few feet away. Gilbreath reached down to retrieve it, and saw with horror that it was broken, snapped completely in two. Useless!

As soon as Dr. Shroeder inhaled the intense reek with his powerful, unprotected nose, he fell to the ground.

"Sniffton! Oh, no!" shrieked Miss Lilly. "Gilbreath, DO SOMETHING!"

Gilbreath knew what to do. It was up to him. He had to save the world from stench. He picked up the packaged peace fragrances carefully. "Let's go, Whiff," he said bravely.

"Woof," Whiff said bravely back.

Chapter Eleven
Fume Face-Off

Gilbreath and Whiff fought their way through the fumes to the alien spaceship. The constant Stink Pot reek surrounded them, filling the air with stench. *Melting Sludge Rot, Spewing Volcano Vomit, Oozing Sleech Scum.* Gilbreath tried to focus on the Odor Decoder printout to keep his mind from blacking out. His odor neutralizer was barely effective.

Gilbreath trudged on, the stench clouding his mind and slowing his steps. Stumbling, he forced himself forward. Stench rolled over him in waves, but he was almost to the space ship entrance. He and Whiff were both crawling by the time they reached the door.

And then, suddenly, there seemed to be a little

relief. A space between the blasting stenches. Gilbreath wasn't sure at first, but there it was again, a space with no odor at all. The alien Stink Pots were coming a little less frequently, the stinkage was noticeably lower. Gilbreath started to breathe a sigh of relief, but then he realized that between each lessening Stink Pot reekage, there was no odor. He ripped off his odor neutralizer and sniffed frantically. Nothing. Nothing pleasant, nothing stinky. Little by little, the Stink Pots grew weaker until there was absolutely no odor at all. Gilbreath could smell nothing.

He tried to keep from panicking.

"Whiff!" he whispered, nose to nose. "I don't smell anything!"

"Woof!" Whiff agreed, his eyes huge with fear.

Had the alien plot succeeded? Was this total odor annihilation?

Gilbreath and Whiff took deep breaths of nothing, and entered the alien spaceship cautiously, holding the peace offering with care. The light inside was dim, but they could see big blobs of trashy garbage all over the spaceship floor. Gilbreath sniffed for more information, but there was still no odor, not even from the huge garbage mounds that looked like they should reek horribly. There was no printout from the Odor Decoder.

Gilbreath and Whiff took a step forward.

Suddenly, one of the garbage piles rolled toward them and lifted up what looked like a huge nose, sniffing the air. The nostrils flared wildly. Gilbreath realized the garbage was alive. The garbage piles were the aliens! "Aaaaah!" he screamed.

"Hooonnkk!" blew the giant nose from the garbage pile. For a split second, Gilbreath was surrounded by a puff of  odor, but it disappeared immediately. The Odor Decoder managed to take a reading: *Alien Nostril Splurge*. Out of curiosity, Gilbreath checked the Odor Emoter, aiming it straight at the garbage pile. The screen said, SURPRISED.

Gilbreath looked closer. The alien's nostrils were huge, like caves, and they flared slowly in and out. He couldn't see any other features. No eyes, no ears. Only a great big nose sticking out of a mound of garbage. Gilbreath looked at Whiff, eyes wide. He tugged at his modest nose and pushed up his glasses. Feeling every emotion from panic to hope, he gathered up all the courage he had, stepped forward, and placed the peace offering under the big alien nose.

Chapter Twelve
A Surprising Reaction

Gilbreath watched the aliens' nostrils flare in and out peacefully. So far the aliens seemed friendly. Gilbreath held his breath as the alien leader leaned its huge nostrils over the white peace bottle.

Suddenly, the gigantic nostrils began flapping and flipping and opening and closing at an amazing speed.

"Does that mean he likes it, Whiff?" wondered Gilbreath.

But in the next instant, the alien leader's nose emitted a loud honk and he fell, unconscious, to the floor of the spaceship. The bottle landed with a thud, and the wonderful peace fragrances went swirling throughout the ship.

One by one, the other aliens' inhaled the lovely fragrances and began flapping, flipping, opening, and rapidly closing their nostrils. Gilbreath and Whiff watched in horror as each alien honked loudly and fell to the floor.

"Oh, no!" Gilbreath said to his pal. "What have we done, Whiff? We tried to save the world, but we ended up with a bunch of passed out aliens! What do we do now?"

As if things weren't bad enough, Gilbreath looked out the spacecraft sky window and saw a black, swirling cloud moving toward the ship.

Suddenly Dr. Shroeder appeared at the alien spaceship door, followed closely by Professor Blink. They had revived as soon as the stench had disappeared.

"Gilbreath! Whiff! Are you all right?" Dr. Shroeder called, blinking into the dimness of the spacecraft. Usually he used his sense of smell first, but since there was no odor at all, he took in the situation by sight. There appeared to be piles of garbage all over the spacecraft floor. When one of the huge nostrils trembled, Dr. Shroeder realized these were the aliens.

"Uncle Shroeder, am I glad to see you!" Gilbreath said with relief. "The peace offering made the aliens pass out, and all the other smells in the world have disappeared!"

"Where is the peace offering?" asked Professor Blink frantically. "Where are the aliens?" He tripped over a pile of garbage and fell facedown into an alien nostril.

"The peace offering caused the aliens to pass out?" Dr. Shroeder repeated thoughtfully. He shined a flashlight and peered into one of the alien nostrils. "These aliens have a high-level sense of smell, but they are structured very differently from us."

Suddenly Gilbreath had an idea. "Uncle Shroeder, do you think the aliens thought the Stink Pots smelled good and that our peace offering smelled terrible? I mean, maybe they were being friendly and the Stink Pots were actually gifts to us. Since our peace fragrance made them pass out, I mean."

"I think you may be correct, Gilbreath," Dr. Shroeder said.

"Our peace offering must have been the worst stench they could imagine. It caused them all to faint. Likewise, their Stink Pots must have been friendly gifts of fragrance to us. It wasn't an evil plot at all."

"But, Uncle Shroeder, there's more," Gilbreath said, pointing to the spaceship window. The frightening black swirl was getting closer.

"Professor Blink, take a look out this window," Dr. Shroeder said.

Professor Blink was still facedown in the alien nostril. "What window? Where's the window?" he said, pulling his head out of the slurge.

Gilbreath gave Professor Blink a hand. "Up here," he said.

Professor Blink emerged, rumpled and slightly damp. "Thank you, Gilbreath." Professor Blink looked up at the sky window and jumped back with a start. "Oh, no!" he said. "It can't be! It's, it's, it's a BLACK HOLE OF ODOR! The horrible smells unleashed by the aliens combined with the Hillbilly Toot 'n' Nanny has created a vacuum that will suck in anything and everything!"

"Professor Blink is clearly correct," confirmed Dr. Shroeder. "That explains why there are no fragrances detectable. The Black Hole has pulled in every smell." The lovely peace offering scents circled and swirled toward the Black Hole. With horror, they felt the spaceship being sucked in, too.

"Somehow, we must revive the aliens, and warn them of the danger," said Dr. Shroeder. "Before their spaceship is pulled into the Black Hole. Quickly, Gilbreath, Whiff! Nose-to-nose resuscitation! And be careful not to fall in!"

Chapter Fourteen
Odor Emotion

Finally the dazed aliens came to, shaking their garbage bodies and flaring their nostrils. Dr. Shroeder tried to explain the dangerous situation, only to realize the aliens had no ears. Gilbreath tried to point out the swirling Black Hole to the leader, but remembered the aliens had no eyes. Professor Blink was still confused about where the aliens were and why the spaceship was so messy. There seemed to be no way to communicate.

Suddenly, Gilbreath had another idea. "Whiff!" he said. "The aliens might not have senses like ours, or understand our language, but I bet there's one way we're alike."

"Woof?" said Whiff.

"They have feelings! Remember how the Emoter told us they were surprised? Uncle Shroeder! Maybe we can communicate with feelings. We'll use the Odor Emoter!" Gilbreath took out the Emoter. He aimed it at the aliens and typed in HAPPY.

It took a minute. The Emoter gurgled and rolled. It bubbled and jumped. Then a sickening odor of moldy rot wafted from Dr. Shroeder's invention. The smell was quickly swirled away, sucked in by the Black Hole of Odor, but not before the aliens got a whiff. Their huge nostrils flared happily, and they seemed to dance for a minute.

"I think it worked!" exclaimed Gilbreath.

"Brilliant idea," his famous uncle said with admiration. "Think, Gilbreath. What emotion will make the aliens leave, and escape the danger?"

They could feel the spacecraft being pulled slowly toward the Black Hole.

"I'll try 'fear,'" said Gilbreath.

He aimed the Emoter at the aliens again and typed FEAR. The Emoter worked faster this time, releasing a light candy scent that the humans found delightful. The Odor Decoder, however, identified it as Angry Crater-monster Sweat. The aliens' nostrils flared and quivered, then they all jumped into hiding places. But they didn't take the spaceship and leave.

"There's got to be a way to get them to go!" Gilbreath said.

"Woof," said Whiff. He put his paw on Gilbreath's knee, then rested his furry head against his pal.

"Do you mean 'friendship,' Whiff? Oh, wait, I know!"

Gilbreath typed in HOMESICKNESS, and pointed it at the aliens.

Unfamiliar odors rolled out, identified by the Odor Decoder as Slurpy Nostril Hugs, Filthy Fireside Fungus, Cozy Cave Crud, Steaming Crater Garbage with Extra Cheese. The aliens turned to each other and began to honk softly.

Their nostrils got drippy, their messy piles drooped. The odors had definitely made them homesick.

The alien leader fired up the spaceship, and the aliens prepared for takeoff. One alien pulled Gilbreath and Whiff into what Gilbreath could only describe as a slurpy nostril hug. It honked a farewell and puffed them with a sudden stench that knocked Gilbreath backward, then the smell was swirled away by the Black Hole.

Dr. Shroeder, Gilbreath, and Whiff jumped out the spacecraft door, pulling Professor Blink with them. They waved good-bye even though they knew the aliens couldn't see.

And then, like an afterthought, a huge suction tube punched out from the side of the alien spacecraft and reached into the center of the Black Hole, like a giant Odor Unloader. It whined and groaned and twisted and curled until it had sucked each alien Stink Pot odor back into the spacecraft. Gilbreath watched the Odor Decoder printout register the fragrances as they went from the Black Hole into the suction tube: *Nasty*

Nebula Gnarl, Grimy Galactic Globules,
Putrid Planetary Plop.

"I guess they decided to take their stinky gifts with them," said Gilbreath, "but they left something else behind. What is that?"

Gilbreath and Whiff took a closer look. The spaceship had left a giant puddle of some gooey substance that resembled lime green slime.

Chapter Fifteen

No Nonscents

The aliens were gone, but the Black Hole remained, holding all the odors it had sucked up from Earth. The Hillbillies, now revived, moped around as if it were the end of the world. Thanks to the Black Hole the camp was boring—there was no odor to be sniffed anywhere.

There was no fresh scent of hay bales for the square dance, no sweet flower nectar from the gardens, no polished wood fragrance as the Hillbillies tuned their fiddles.

There was no smoky scent from the campfire, no obnoxious reek from the outhouse, no woodsy aroma from the autumn leaves. There was no reason to smellabrate at all. No toot in the Toot 'n' Nanny.

The Black Hole swirled overhead. Professor

Blink wandered around, looking at the sky, analyzing the Black Hole with his pocket smelloscope, pocket calculator, and pocket pen, all of which he seemed surprised to find in his pocket.

"Uncle Shroeder, this is terrible!" said Gilbreath. "No odor at all is worse even than terrible stench. We have to do something."

"You are correct, Gilbreath," agreed Dr. Shroeder. He thought for a moment. "The aliens were able to pull their odors out of the Black Hole with their powerful space tube. If only I could make the Odor Unloader strong enough to suck the remaining odors out and return them to their rightful locations! But we tried it at the Space Scenter, and the Unloader wasn't powerful enough."

Gilbreath was busy studying the yellow-green pool of lime slime left behind by the spaceship. It was thick, slick, and sticky. Something about it was familiar. Suddenly, he knew what it was. "Uncle Shroeder! I know how the aliens made their suction tube work so well! They used the same secret fuel additive that makes the snotomobile run! That means this gooey green slime puddle is a huge pool of alien—"

"We must hurry!" Professor Blink interrupted. "My calculations show that we have very little time before the Black Hole collapses and all the fragrances are sucked into space!"

Gilbreath quickly pulled the huge Odor Unloader from the snotomobile trunk. He was surprised when Moose, the Sniff-Off champion and Top Tooter, helped him carry the contraption without a word. They hooked up the Odor Unloader, filled it with the secret fuel additive the alien spaceship had left behind, aimed it into the eye of the Black Hole, and turned it up to high.

"Thanks," Gilbreath said to Moose. But Moose was already heading for the barn.

"Nice guy," Gilbreath said to Whiff.

"Woof!" Whiff said, wagging his tail.

Chapter Sixteen
Odor Is Restored

The Odor Unloader pulled fragrances from the Black Hole one by one.

"Great thinking, Gilbreath!" Dr. Shroeder praised his nephew. "The secret fuel additive left behind by the aliens has increased Odor Unloader power by one hundred percent!"

The Odor Decoder identified the scents as they flew out to their correct places: Autumn Leaves, Red Barn Paint, Bare Feet, Baked Beans, Straw Hat, Corncob Pipe . . .

Last, but not least, came the fragrant gift that Gilbreath had bravely taken to the aliens as a peace offering. Gilbreath quickly captured it in a clean bottle before it had a chance to fly off. "Hey, Whiff!" he said happily. "It smells like we can still enter the Sniff-Off!"

"Woof!" wagged Whiff.

They glanced toward the red barn. Kids were standing proudly by their odor bottles, waiting for the judges. Gilbreath saw Moose, covered with blue ribbons, waiting beside the largest bottle on the table.

"Let's get entered," suggested Gilbreath. They went to the judges' stand. The Scent Society ladies gave them a spot right beside Moose.

All around them, people were gearing up for a real smellabration. Gilbreath inhaled the tinge of metal from the Ferris wheel, the tang of barbecue, and the fragrance of sweet watermelon. Hawkers called from game booths, screams and

laughter came from the roller coaster.

The sun was getting lower, and Gilbreath could smell the square dance starting. The fiddles were warming up, and the caller was telling people to find their partners. All in all, the mood was one of happy smellabration and fun.

Gilbreath checked the Odor Emoter to make sure it hadn't overloaded. He was surprised to detect the powdery sugar scent of candy conversation hearts, the muted fragrance of Valentine lace, the delicious aroma of a heart-shaped box of chocolates. He checked the Emoter screen. LOVE?

He looked around in confusion.

Just then, the Scent Society judges came by. They daintily sniffed each entry and made marks on their notepads with white-gloved hands. Then they made an announcement.

"For the fifth year in a row, the winner is, Miss Moose Haybale!"

Gilbreath looked with surprise at the kid standing next to him, the kid who had won the Sniff-Off five years running, the kid who was last year's Top Tooter, the kid who had helped him carry the

Unloader, the kid who was a GIRL! Moose took off her hat, causing two long braids to tumble to her shoulders. She smiled at Gilbreath.

"Whiff!" Gilbreath whispered urgently, nose to nose with his pal. "Moose is a girl!"

"Woof," Whiff said calmly.

"You knew it all along?" said Gilbreath.

Whiff nudged the Emoter softly with his wet muzzle.

Gilbreath inhaled Chocolate-covered Cherries, Fresh Flower Bouquets, and Lace Doilies. He realized the Emoter was pointing straight at Moose.

"A girl who likes me?" Gilbreath said, making a face. "Oh, no!"

At that moment, the fiddles struck up a square dance tune. "Swing your partner, round and round!" Rip Corncob called with enthusiasm.

Gilbreath saw Professor Blink spinning happily around the dance floor with his lab coat flying. Dr. Shroeder danced by with, of all people, Miss Lilly! Gilbreath noticed she was carrying her pink gas mask in case the Toot 'n' Nanny got out of hand. Everyone was smellabrating!

"Grab your partner, Gilbreath!" Dr. Shroeder called.

"Well, I, er . . . ," said Gilbreath. Whiff nudged him toward Moose with his wet nose.

Gilbreath looked at his pal. "No way, Whiff," he said.

Suddenly Moose grabbed Gilbreath by the hand. "I got my partner!" she yelled with glee, her smile revealing the chipped front tooth. Moose skipped to the middle of the square dance floor, pulling a reluctant Gilbreath behind her.

"Yee haw!" they heard Rip Corncob call. "It's a toe-tapper of a square dance tonight! And here come the young 'uns!"

"Whiiiiff!" yelled Gilbreath.

Chapter Seventeen
An Unexpected Reek

"**W**hat a terrific smellabration that was last night!" Gilbreath exclaimed to his uncle and his trusty bloodhound the next morning.

They were relaxing in the backyard of their fragrant cedar cabin high in the mountains. They had to camp out because the cabin was being fumigated after the Toot 'n' Nanny smellabration. "Hot air rises, you know," Dr. Shroeder had explained. They were thankful for the breezes and fresh air.

"Even Miss Lilly joined in!" Gilbreath said with amazement.

"You and Miss Haybale seemed to be enjoying yourselves," Dr. Shroeder said.

"We sure did! Moose is a great square dancer,

a super snozbee player, and she was the Top
Tooter again this year!" Gilbreath stopped,
remembering the toot competition. "Wasn't
Moose amazing? She didn't even make a noise!
But the result was a real stinker." They all
flinched at the memory. "The judges could
hardly breathe. She scored a perfect ten!"

"Silent, but deadly," mused Dr. Shroeder. "A
very clever strategy by Miss Haybale. You
weren't disappointed that your Sniff-Off entry
didn't win first place?"

"A little." Gilbreath pushed up his glasses. "I should have remembered to take out Professor Blink's favorites: Starched Lab Coat and New Graph Paper. Anyway, I did help save the world from odor annihilation. Mr. Corncob says whatever we do in life, we should always toot our own horns. That's why Moose wears her blue ribbons everywhere she goes."

"Really? And did Rip Corncob give you any other words of wisdom?" Dr. Shroeder asked.

"He sure did, Uncle Shroeder," said Gilbreath. "He said that you won a few Toot 'n' Nanny competitions in your time, and that whatever you say, I shouldn't pull your finger."

"I see," chuckled Dr. Shroeder.

Gilbreath and Whiff tossed the snozbee back and forth, lazily. As usual, Dr. Shroeder was going through the mail.

"Here's a postcard from your parents, Gilbreath," he said. "Where are they now?"

Gilbreath closed his eyes and sniffed the scentiment. He could identify the fragrance of tulips in bloom, the fresh breeze of a spinning windmill, the polished scent of wooden shoes.

"Holland?" he guessed, opening his eyes and pushing up his glasses. "I'm right!"

"You know, Gilbreath, the Toot 'n' Nanny was such a success, they will be fumigating our cabin for weeks. Why don't we do a little traveling ourselves?"

"Great, Uncle Shroeder! Where do you want to go?"

Dr. Shroeder picked up a brochure from the mail pile. "How about this?" he said.

The gigantic noses of elephants, rhinoceroses, and other animals were pictured on the brochure. Gilbreath pulled his own nose. "An African sniffari!" he exclaimed. "Cool!"

Whiff sailed the snozbee over Gilbreath's head, into a lilac bush. Gilbreath started to go in after it, but he remembered a lesson he had learned earlier. "I'll sniff before I leap, Whiff," he said. He took a deep breath, but he could detect only the perfume of blooming lilacs, the rich fragrance of damp dirt, and one other odor coming from something squishy just under his shoe—

"Whiff!" he yelled.

"Woof," apologized Whiff.

The horrendous stink of angry skunk came spraying from the bush with no warning. Gilbreath, Whiff, and Dr. Shroeder dove into their tent and zipped the door flap, but the reek penetrated the tent walls.

"Well, that settles it," Dr. Shroeder said. "We'll leave for the sniffari right away."

"Right away is not soon enough," Gilbreath said, holding his nose with both hands, his eyes watering. "Are there skunks in Africa, Uncle Shroeder?"